Daybreak

D1079419

Written by Ally Kennen
Illustrated by Liz Monahan

Collins

Chapter 1

I'm not giving in without a fight. Tomorrow's my birthday
and I'm going to be 12 years old. Surely that gives me rights?

"We're not going to make it to the river. I'm so sorry,"
repeats Mum, her fingers worrying at a loose button on
her cardigan.

"But we'll MISS it," I yell. I can foresee a great deal more
yelling and howling in the next 24 hours.

"There'll be other times, Linnie," says Dad, pulling on his
muddy boots.

"There'll *never* be another five-star bore on my birthday,"
I fume.

Bores are the wrong name for them. There's nothing boring about a huge tidal wall of water piling down the estuary, high as a house, and dotted with crazy surfers, all mad keen to ride the wave until it swallows them up in its foaming brown jaws.

Dad reaches over and rubs my head with his scratchy, calloused hand. "The vet can only come tomorrow morning," he says. "Please try to understand."

I understand all right. Our cows have to be tested for a disease called tuberculosis. And all my birthday plans have been cancelled. I shake Dad off, and he and Mum swap their special, extra-weary "isn't-Linnie-a-pest" look. This look occurs, on average, about four times a day.

"Why can't we move the cows tonight?" I moan. "Then there might be time tomorrow and ..."

"It's not safe. It's too dark," says Dad. "We'll move them first thing in the morning."

"Sorry, Linnie," says Mum again. "If we'd heard from the vet earlier, we might've been able to arrange something. But he's only just called and ..."

"The TB test's at 11 o'clock tomorrow," I mutter. "The cows always ruin everything."

This is what's happened. Two months ago, one of our cows failed her TB test. She had to be put down, and now all our cows have to be tested again. Mum says it's the law. We can't sell any of our cows until all their results come back clean. That means no money. That's why it's so serious. And that's why all my moaning and whingeing won't make any difference.

"Please try to be grown up about it," pleads Mum.

"How can I grow up if I don't get a proper birthday?"

"I've got to take some water up to the sheep," Dad says, scattering mud on the kitchen tiles as he makes for the door. He hates it when I erupt like this, but I can't help myself. I'm so disappointed, I feel like I've been kicked. Kuri, our dog, gets up from under Dad's chair and stretches. She follows Dad out into the farmyard.

Annabelle, my sister, smirks at me from the nook so I throw a cushion at her head. She catches it between her horrible witch-purple fingernails.

"You're such a child," she says.

Annabelle is 13. We share a bedroom and it drives us both mad. Right now, she's looking very pleased because she never wanted to go to the bore anyway.

"I'm supposed to be going shopping with Dottie," she'd moaned only this morning, before the vet called and ruined everything.

"We're all going," Mum had said firmly. "You'll enjoy it once you get there."

"I won't," muttered Annabelle. "I wish I didn't have to go."

Now her wish had come true. Like a bad fairy, she'd put a spell on my birthday.

"Witch," I snarl at her, and throw another cushion. Annoyingly, she catches that one too.

I can feel the tremble coming on; that embarrassing tremble that comes just before a fit of crying. Mum must notice this because she tries to give me a hug but I shoot off round the kitchen table before she can reach me.

"It's not FAIR," I shout. "This stupid farm is *always* more important than *me*."

"This farm *is* more important than you," says Annabelle, smugly.

Mum starts to say something to me, but I've heard enough. In five seconds, I've crossed the kitchen floor and I'm racing up the stairs. I run to the bathroom, lock the door and blast on the bath taps. I watch the water whirl down the plughole. I hope the crash of water against the enamel will drown out the sound of my sobbing. I don't want Annabelle to hear.

This is going to be the worst birthday ever.

Chapter 2

I'm too angry to sleep. I'm lying in bed, and my thoughts are spinning round and round my head like a washing machine.

I first saw a tidal bore last spring. It was registered as a two-star event, which is small compared with tomorrow's five-star bore. Even so, last year was brilliant. We'd walked up the river to a place where the bank sloped gently down. Out of nowhere, the water piled down the river in a steep wave, making the ground shake and shudder under my feet. Dad had to grab my arm and yank me back. If I hadn't moved, I would've been swept away. The water broke off overhanging branches, and clumps of the bank just collapsed into the water. Mum went pale – I don't think she'd expected the bore to be quite so fast and big. We all got soaked in the spray as the wave roared past. I've never seen anything so powerful and exciting as that wave.

Tomorrow's bore will be the biggest of the year; mightier than any I've seen before. Helicopters will be hovering and TV cameras will be filming. In the river there'll be surfers, people on canoes and even swimmers. Crowds of people will line the banks, and there'll be ice-cream vans, hot dog stands and balloon-sellers. People will be taking photographs and selling souvenirs. And the fantastic thing is that this five-star, totally amazing phenomenon is happening on my birthday. This makes it even more magical, like nature has programmed it just for me.

I hear Annabelle turn over in her sleep. There's a silver line taped down the centre of the carpet. One half of the room is Annabelle's, and the other belongs to me. We don't cross the line. I've put my bookcase right up against the line, and Annabelle has her dressing table a bit further down.
Mum says it's crazy to have our furniture in the centre of the room. We both disagree with her. Sometimes, Annabelle and I discuss the possibility of building a proper partition, with wood and plasterboard. That, at least, would stop the mean comments, the hairbrushes, tissues and socks, which fly over the line in both directions, but Mum says a wall isn't practical.

What I hate most about Annabelle is how she completely ignores me at school, like I'm the most embarrassing thing ever. Annabelle thinks she's so grown up, but she's only 14 months older than I am, which is nothing. And I also hate how when she has her friends Dottie and Sash round, they whisper for hours, and giggle and give me evil looks. I'm not allowed to join in. They call themselves the Three Tops, and they think they are *it*.

Annabelle and I used to get on. I remember us sitting on the wall killing ourselves laughing as we watched Dad hopping round the yard trying to catch one of his sheep. That was only a few years ago. Now all she wants to do is talk to Dottie and Sash on the phone.

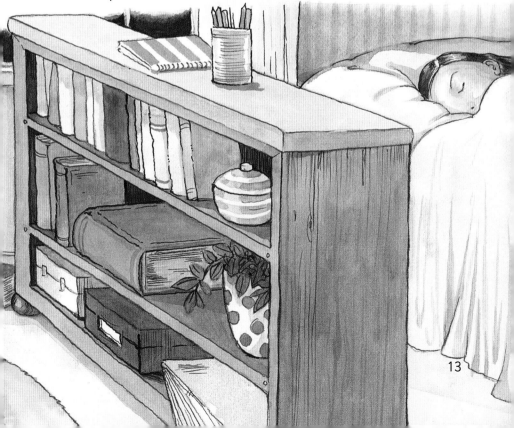

I hear a little cough in the darkness.

"Let's hope Angel passes her test," Annabelle's voice sneaks out from behind the bookcase, "because we know what'll happen if she doesn't."

Sisters can be cruel. Mine is crueller than most.

"Shut up," I snarl.

Angel is my favourite cow. She's one of the boss cows. She's a big, strong, silvery-white animal with dark, wet eyes and a pink nose. I saw her being born; a slippery bundle of legs. When she came out, she wasn't breathing and Dad gave me a handful of straw and told me to rub her wet back. I sat in the dark cow shed, trying to rub some life into this floppy new creature. After a minute or two, when I was beginning to think it wasn't going to work, the little calf coughed and breathed and shook her head. And everything was all right. Maybe I saved Angel's life, maybe I didn't. I was given the honour of naming her, and I called her Angel, because that was how she seemed to me – a new, bright, beautiful life. A miracle.

Angel grew up on the farm and has become one of our suckler cows. We breed from her. All the other cows respect Angel and walk behind her, and when I was smaller, she used to let me ride on her back, down from the fields.

"Dead," whispers Annabelle in a throaty voice. "Slaughtered."

I throw my slipper in her direction. Then I turn over in bed and look out of the window at the night. There's a big, big moon in the sky. Years ago, Annabelle and I agreed to have the curtains open whenever there was a full moon in order to soak up the moon rays while we slept.

Moon rays give you magical powers.

It's this big old moon that will be responsible for tomorrow's five-star bore.

There'll be a spring tide tomorrow, at nine-thirty a.m. It's like fate. There's been a big wind and the waves will be huge. It'll feel like a festival on the river banks, with people coming from miles around, stepping out of their lives for a few hours to watch something incredible.

But not me.

I listen to Annabelle breathing, so quietly she's almost not there. This is her awake breathing. I wait. Gradually her breathing slows, then it gets noisier. This is her asleep breathing.

I shut my eyes and imagine myself turning off a switch in my head.

The downstairs clock chimes. It's five in the morning. I've been asleep, but now I'm wide awake. I realise I'm no longer 11 years old.

Goodbye 11. It's a little bit sad, but also exciting.

I get out of bed and look out of the window at the farmyard. It's still dark out there, but it won't be for long. The big barn stands empty, the metal roof creaking in the wind.

I'm going out.

17

Chapter 3

I slink along the landing and down the stairs. In the back porch, Kuri's already awake; she must've heard me coming. As she rises from her basket, I smell damp, worried dog. Poor Kuri, she lost her old friend, Toots, last winter. Toots was our old farm dog and she was so good with the livestock. She could have won prizes in sheepdog competitions, Mum said. But just before Christmas, she started being sick all the time and we found some lumps on her tummy. She was pretty old and she had to be put down, but I was only a little bit sad. Toots wasn't very friendly and she had red-rimmed, rheumy eyes. She slept outside and she growled a lot, showing her sharp yellow teeth. She wasn't a people-dog: she bit strange men, like the gate salesman and the man who delivers the cattle feed. But Kuri really missed her at first. She kept waiting at the gate for Toots to come in from the fields. And it's much harder for Kuri to round up the cows and sheep on her own.

I slip on my boots. Dad's dirty overalls reek of cow dung, which mingles with the bright perfume of the spilt washing powder on the cold, tiled floor.

As I step outside, I'm satisfied that nobody knows where I am. I may hide for hours.

The yard's wet from last night's rain, and the moon wavers in the puddles. Kuri trots behind me, tail curled in. She doesn't like getting up this early.

I walk down the ramp to the cattle shed, and squeeze through the gap between the buildings. The sheds are still full of dung, as the cows have only just gone back outside after the winter.

There are 45 stirks in the meadow. The stirks are our young cows that were born last year. Dad'll round them up in a few hours' time on his quad bike, with Kuri. He'll bring them into the big barn. Then at high tide time, we'll all be roped in to go up the lanes to the high field to bring in Angel and the rest of the suckler herd. There are about 30 of them. We'll walk the cows down the road, and any cars will have to crawl behind us.

But it's easy enough as all the cows will follow Angel.

Then we'll pen the cows in the yard and wheel out the cattle crush – the special cage that keeps the cows safe while they're being inspected. And at 11 o'clock, Anthony the vet will come and start the blood tests.

Happy birthday, Linnie.

Before I slide into the forest, I look up, behind the house and beyond the road to the high fields. Dawn light is just beginning to streak the sky and I think I can make out the bulky shapes of the cows, meandering over the grass up there. And there's a white shape floating near the hedge. That can only be Angel.

We only took the cows up there last week. I love it when cows get let out for the spring. They go berserk. You see full-grown cows gambol around like calves, with great fat sides heaving, and hooves pounding as they burn around faster than you think a cow should run. It's like the beginning of the summer holidays for them.

I think I'll go and have a word with Angel.

So here I am, streaming up the hill with the wind behind me. Kuri keeps close. Sometimes I'm afraid of the dark, sometimes I'm not. Now I'm definitely not. I feel like I'm part of the darkness. This is bad of me. I'm not supposed to sneak out without anyone knowing where I am. But it is morning, after all, though the sun hasn't come up yet.

I'm flying up the farm track, then I cut over the field to the lane. I'm not cold. I feel wide awake, and in about 15 minutes I'm panting at the gate of the high field.

"Angel," I call.

I smell hot dung and damp hair, wafting over the field. The cattle are standing and sitting under the hedge in the far corner.

Kuri presses her wet nose into my hand. She loves me best out of the whole family. This makes Annabelle mad. But if you want to get a dog to like you, you have to feed it and take it for walks. Annabelle says the smell of dog food makes her sick and she doesn't like getting muddy. So Kuri is mine, but tomorrow, or rather later this morning, she'll turn into Kuri the farm dog. It's like she's got a split personality. One minute, she'll be licking my boots, the next she'll be snapping and snarling at the cows' heels to get them to go where she wants.

I lean on the gate and give a little shiver. The bore will sweep past in four-and-a-half hours. If only the cows were already in the yard, we might have time for the trip to the river before the vet comes. It's so exciting, watching the bore-water crest down the river. And the West Country surf champion, Toby Eggers, is going to try and surf down it! I've got pictures of him all over my half of the room. Even Annabelle doesn't mind them.

But, of course, I'm going to miss all of this.

A ghostly shape lumbers up the field and two shining eyes look into mine. It's Angel.

"It's you and your mates' fault," I grumble, scratching her ears. "I wish you'd all just take yourselves down into the yard."

Angel smells lovely, like warm grass and wet hair. She butts at the gate with her head. It looks like she's trying to unlatch the gate herself.

Then I have a thought. Just suppose, when Mum and Dad get up this morning, they find the cows are already waiting in the yard. That'd leave us time to see the bore. It's only 16 kilometres to the river. It could be done. A prickle of excitement runs down my back. We'd be back before Anthony, the vet, arrived.

It's about two-and-a-half kilometres down the lane to the farm gate. And there wouldn't be any traffic about at this hour. The lane stretches silver-grey behind me. Very soon it'll be dawn.

Just suppose …

I don't stop to think too much. Kuri gives a low growl as Angel bumps the gate again and I reach over and unhook the metal clasp.

The gate swings open.

Chapter 4

Angel looks at me, then tosses her head and gives a long loud bellow.

"To the farm," I tell Kuri. "Good girl, to the farm." Kuri has herded the cows down this lane a thousand times before. I'll just have to guide in the stragglers at the back.

But then things start to happen very fast. One minute the cows are all lumped in the far corner of the field, chewing the cud, sleeping or quietly grazing, the next, there's a thunder of hooves. A dark river of cows flows down the hill towards me as Angel gives another bellow and pushes past me into the lane. It's like she's got the devil in her. I feel a bolt of alarm. Maybe this wasn't such a good idea, after all. I start to close the gate, but it's too late. The cows have got the wind behind them and their big, heavy bodies push back the gate, pressing me into the hedge and making it impossible to shut it.

Then I hear Kuri, barking wildly. It's a short, cross bark. The cows are stampeding up the road, bucking and trotting and kicking out their legs. The air is full of flies and noise and droplets of mud.

I see Angel at the front of the pack, running up the hill. I clamp my hand over my mouth.

The cows are going in the wrong direction.

They mustn't go up the hill as it leads to a crossroads. Here, one road leads to our neighbour's farm. The other road goes down to the meadows and the third way, straight on, is a small lane which, after a kilometre or so, leads steeply down into the very centre of town.

"KURI," I yell. "GET ROUND!" Kuri chases on to the verge, trying to get through the throng to the front, but when the cows sense the dog at their heels, they run faster.

"GET ROUND, KURI!" I scream, as the little dog disappears under a sea of tails and hooves and cows' backsides. But she's not having any luck. She needs Toots to back her up. But Toots isn't here any more.

29

Just then I hear a deep bellow, one that sends a rush of fear down my back. I look back into the field at the remaining cows and see, to my alarm, a shape, bigger than most, hulking down the hill at a million miles an hour.

I'd completely forgotten that Behemoth, the bull, was in the field with the cows.

Behemoth is a nine-year-old tonne of beef. He has an unpredictable personality. Sometimes he's the softest and meekest animal on the farm, but at other times he can be very pushy. He can get all snorty, and he throws his weight around, and that's when we children are told to get out of the way. I have to admit I'm quite scared of him. Farm girls aren't supposed to be scared of bulls, but I don't walk through a field if I know he's in there.

Once, when I was six years old, he came rampaging into the yard, bellowing and mooing. I didn't know where Dad was, but Mum was calling my name, calling for me to get in the house. But I couldn't, because I was hiding behind the henhouse and I didn't want Behemoth to see me. There was only a thin fence separating the chickens from the yard, easy for Behemoth to knock down, and I was so scared that I crawled in through the tiny hatch into the henhouse and curled up as small as I could, in all the straw, with chicken manure soaking into my trousers. I listened to Behemoth roar and the thin wood of the henhouse seemed to tremble. I didn't move a muscle as he crashed past. Mum hates me telling this story. She said she'd no idea where I was, because I hid there for a whole hour, long after the bull had crashed out of the yard and into the meadow to the other cattle. I remember finally crawling out, poking my head out of the hole, terrified that the bull was outside waiting for me.

Dad says Behemoth's all right really, it's just you wouldn't want him bumping into you if he was in a hurry to get somewhere. Right now, he's in a hurry to get out of the gate. I'm 41 kilograms. He's over 1,000 kilograms. I don't wish to die, especially on my twelfth birthday, so I jump backwards into the hedge, pressing myself into the brambles as he thunders past and out into the road.

He charges up the lane after the others. I think he's annoyed that his wives have gone off without him. He shoulders his way through the crowd, towards the front. Behemoth is mostly content to run in the pack and let Angel lead, but sometimes, like now, he wants to be in front. As I watch the hooves flying, clattering on the road, tails swishing and cowpats splattering on the tarmac, I'm frozen with fear. My parents are going to go nuts. I'm in the biggest trouble of my life.

Just then, the gate is wrenched out from under my arms and clicks shut as the last few cows gallop up to it.

"What are you doing, Linnie?" screeches a high-pitched voice. "Have you gone mad?"

Annabelle, my sister, hangs on the gate, panting. I'm so astonished I can't say a word.

This has turned into a double nightmare.

Chapter 5

"Come on!" yells Annabelle. She grabs me roughly and drags me up the hill after the cows. "If we don't stop them, they'll be into the town."

I can see the backs of the last two cows disappear round the corner at the top of the hill. Annabelle's right. There's no time to get Mum and Dad.

"What're you doing here?" I splutter as we run up the road. "It's 5.30 in the morning."

"Why are *you* here?" breathes Annabelle. She's wearing wellies pulled over her pyjamas and Mum's big old cardigan round her shoulders like a cape. "Why did you open that gate? You let Behemoth out! He might KILL someone."

I don't know what to say.

"Run faster," orders Annabelle.

My lungs hurt and I'm tired. We'll never catch them up. I feel another crying shiver come over me. Annabelle saw me open the gate, which means I'm done for. I'm surprised she's helping me at all.

It's getting lighter all the time. The sky is now a deep blue, with rivers of orange and pink running along the horizon. At the top of the hill, we can see far down the lane. The cows are a black mass, careering off the verges and bellowing.

There must be about 30 of them, including Behemoth.

"They've gone mad," says Annabelle. Vainly I look for Kuri.
I hope she's all right under all those hooves.

We run up the hill after them. I pray no cars or tractors or people are coming the other way. I run, skidding on cowpats and letting out frightened little sobs. All the time Annabelle is breathlessly demanding what I was thinking, and telling me how stupid I am, and how Dad is the only person who should handle Behemoth, and how I'm going to get done. I wonder what would happen if Annabelle and I just stopped running and slipped quietly home and into bed, and in the morning we'd say we'd no idea how the cows got out. But as soon as the idea crosses my mind I blank it out.

I've started all this and if I don't stop it, someone might get hurt. I pull myself together, and run on.

We're beginning to catch up. The cows, although mooing and grunting, have slowed to a trot. Cows don't really like running, not for long. Annabelle has caught up with the stragglers – she was always a faster runner than me – and I'm not far behind. I hear a yapping from the front of the pack. Kuri is still trying to head them off.

But now we're getting close to the crossroads. I try to get up on the verge to slip past, but the closer I get, the faster the cows run.

"I'll try this way!" shouts Annabelle, and she climbs the gate into the field that runs alongside the road. I can see what she's planning – she's going to run along the field to get ahead of the herd, then jump out in front of them. The cows must be getting tired too. I manage to overtake a couple of stragglers at the back. I recognise Celandine and Jackaranda. These two are quite old now, and don't like running. I weave through the cows, gradually overtaking them. They smell hot, and steam rises from their backs.

"Only me," I sing soothingly as I push through. As we crest the hill, I see I'm close to the leaders who are beating along at a fair pace. There's Angel's silvery back and just behind her, the big powerful shoulders of Behemoth. They're racing; each one wants to be in front. Behemoth is cross – he's doing his dangerous snort. Usually, if we hear this snort, even Dad gets out of Behemoth's way until the bull has calmed down.

The crossroads is only 100 metres or so ahead. The white metal signpost shines in the dawn light, with arms pointing in four directions.

I'm praying that the cows won't go straight on, where the lane funnels and grows narrow and leads down into our town. I'm only a few metres behind Behemoth now, but how am I going to stop them? For the millionth time, I wish I'd never opened that gate.

As we approach the crossroads, Angel and Behemoth slow down. They seem to be deciding which way to go. Summoning up all my courage, I run on the verge to overtake them. As I pass Angel, Kuri shoots out from behind me and skips around ahead of Behemoth. She lets out a series of short yaps. She's scared: her tail is between her legs and her ears are flat against her head. But Behemoth just lets out a warning bellow.

"Get out of it, Kuri!" I shriek and the little dog skitters out of the way. Behemoth grunts and heads straight on, towards town. But as he passes the signpost, a small figure darts out of the hedge and stands right in his path.

Annabelle!

The inside of my mouth goes all funny as I watch Behemoth thundering towards my sister. Annabelle looks tiny, standing there in the middle of the road. She's holding a thin stick, which wouldn't stop a bird, let alone a Behemoth.

She can't move. I can see her white face, just a blur. Now she's even dropped the stick.

If she doesn't get out of the way, she'll be killed. I screw my face up in horror. "Annabelle!" I scream, sick with fear. "NO!"

As she stands there, a pheasant flies hooting out of the hedge and Behemoth bellows and lunges forward.

I don't stop to think. Instead, I push away my fear, and I dart forwards and grab Annabelle's arm. I drag her up into the hedge, crashing us into the brambles, as Behemoth thunders past, snorting and grunting, his eyes glinting, with the rest of the herd pounding behind him.

They're heading straight towards the town.

"I didn't think he was going to stop," I say apologetically, as Annabelle rubs her arm where I'd held her.

"Maybe not," she says in a quiet voice.

Chapter 6

Ackley is a small town with one long high street and lots of roads leading off it. From the air, it must look like a giant insect. We've got a school, two small supermarkets, a garage, a chip shop and three more small, gifty sort of shops. There's a war memorial in the centre and an octagonal, cobbled, covered building which is hundreds of years old and used to be a wool market. It's on all the postcards of our town.

It's no place for cows.

"They're slowing down," says Annabelle. We're both exhausted. Something has changed between us. She's no longer yelling at me and telling me what a loser I am.

Maybe it's because I've just saved her life.

And I'm feeling different about her too. She's always been my big sister, my big, all-powerful sister, but back then, under the nose of Behemoth, she'd looked tiny.

I'd never thought of Annabelle as being tiny before.

The first houses of the town come into view and my sister gives me a nod.

Just before the town there's a wide verge; it's our plan to get ahead of the cows there. We're hoping they'll stop to eat and relax a little. If one of them calms down, they all will, and maybe Behemoth will fall in with the herd again and stop his battle with Angel for supremacy.

At first the plan seems to work. The cows jump off the road, one by one, on to the verge and blow out their flanks. Steam rises from them. Angel, bless her, puts her head down and starts eating and Behemoth, glad of the rest, does the same. Annabelle and I race along the lane and finally get ahead. Behemoth lifts his massive head and watches us, but he's calmed right down.

That's when I see the open gate. It leads to the back garden of the big pink house on the corner.

"Up round, Kuri," I call, and the little dog once again whips to the head of the pack. "Head him round!" I yell, gesturing at the bull, who's now looking confused rather than angry.

"What're you doing?" screams Annabelle from somewhere within the thicket of cows. "That's Dottie's garden."

"So, she'll understand," I yell, and I skip sideways and give Behemoth a massive whack on his huge behind, as Kuri heads him off and he bounces into the garden together with two of his favourite wives, the hugely fat Lady Porridge and the devious Skylark.

I hang on the gate and fly it shut. The latch closes with a satisfying click.

Just for safety, I loop the string around the post. Behemoth, Skylark and Lady Porridge immediately put their heads down and start eating the lawn.

"It's lucky that Dottie's family haven't mown the grass," I say.

Annabelle appears beside me, white-faced. "Linnie," she snaps. "IDIOT."

And to my surprise, she bursts into tears and turns and heads off after the rest of the cows.

"But I've isolated the bull; the rest should be easy," I shout after her. "Dottie will understand, won't she?"

I charge after my sister. We're too late. Angel is leading
everyone bang smack into the town. But at least they're all
going at a more sedate pace now that Angel isn't
racing Behemoth.

"Oh no!" I groan.

We watch helplessly as Mirage noses the petrol pumps at
the garage, knocking one pump right out of the machine.
Mrs Willowby scratches herself against the bus shelter.

As the day lightens, we see Geraldine stare, transfixed,
at her murky reflection in the newsagent's window, and brown
and white Precious nibble the marigolds in the planters on
the gift-shop windowsill. The whole street gleams with steaming
cowpats. Anthea has got a wrapper of chips out of the bin and
Dazzler is systematically kicking over a row of boxes of recycling.
Luckily, there's no one about. But I'm aware someone might
wake up at any minute, or the milkman might appear.
We have to hurry.

"But why are you so cross?" I ask, hurrying after Annabelle to the front. "Dottie's your friend, isn't she?"

"Get off!" Annabelle slaps at Midnight's side as the cow is about to climb the steps of the war memorial. My sister spins round to face me. She's breathing fast and somewhere during the chase she's lost Mum's cardigan.

"My name will be MUD after this," says Annabelle, watching as a light goes on above the newsagent's. "Why did you have to pick Dottie's garden?"

I stare, not sure I understand.

"The Three Tops just don't *do* stuff like this," says Annabelle. "We always act normal. We *never* do anything embarrassing. Dottie will go nuts."

We're ahead of the pack now and the cows have come to a complete halt. Kuri keeps them back, snarling and growling if one tries to step forward.

"I don't get it," I say bemused. "Dottie's your best friend. Surely she'll understand."

"We'll be laughed at in school. And so will Dottie and she'll blame me. You have to earn your place to be in the Three Tops. We're the most normal girls in the year."

I don't get all this *normal* stuff. "Why is being normal so important?"

"If you aren't normal, you stand out," says Annabelle, and she steps forward. "Come on, let's get out of here."

I watch as she shoos the cows round. They've had enough, by the look of it; they're all standing around, breathing hard and mooing gently.

Annabelle orders me to the front, to walk with Angel, and she says she'll bring up the rear.

"Are we really going to do this?" I ask, as I scramble round. I've lost all confidence in my cattle-moving skills.

Annabelle nods grimly.

The cows form a rough line and amble off back in the direction of the farm. A car pulls out of a side road. I know who it is – Mr Fox who drives 100 kilometres every day to his job in the city. His daughter's in my class. They only moved here recently.

"Everything all right?" he asks, looking bemused.

"Fine," says Annabelle, and she addresses the cows. "Move on."

Mr Fox gingerly manoeuvres his big red car out of the side street and slides up the road behind us. The wheels spin through a slick of cowpat and a wild giggle builds up in me.

"Shouldn't we have asked him for help?" I call back to my sister, who is urging on the cows at the back.

"Just GO!" she shouts. "Everything'll be fine now."

But of course, it isn't.

Chapter 7

I check my watch and it's just after six. As we leave the town,
I feel a huge sense of relief. No shop windows have been smashed.
No cows have run away. I'm jogging at a smart pace back up
the road, with the cows walking behind me. I'm still in trouble,
I know that, but we've got the situation under control. Just.
Dad would have to come back for Behemoth, but I'd work out
what to say later. My breathing slows and the pounding in my
chest recedes. As I walk, I steal a look at Annabelle, walking at
the back. Her shiny hair bounces off her shoulders as she walks.
She has to be normal? Just to be with her friends? That sounds hard.
Maybe things aren't so easy for her, after all.

As I pass Dottie's house, Behemoth is standing at the gate,
leaning over the railings.

I look back at Annabelle. "Do you really want me to let
him out?" I call. "Just so Dottie doesn't see?"

"No!" she shouts. "It's TOO LATE. Just keep going."
She looks anxiously at the curtains in the bedroom windows.

"She'll understand … ow!" A huge pressure slams into my leg.
There's a blinding pain. I can't stand up. I topple over into
the hedge, clutching my shin. Samantha, one of the really bossy
cows who vies with Angel for top position, has just bashed me. I sit
on the verge, groaning and rubbing my leg. Tears come to my eyes.

Up front, the cows stop and nose the hedge for something to eat.

"WHAT NOW?" shouts Annabelle from the back.

"My leg," I moan. "I can't walk."

There's a silence, at least, as much of a silence as there can be with 30 cows stomping around and munching grass and coughing and grunting. Cows are noisy, even when they're being quiet.

"MOVE!" yells Annabelle. Over her head I can see a van coming up the lane behind us. But my leg is excruciating.

I just sit and wait for the pain to subside.

"RIDE ANGEL THEN!" screams Annabelle.

"But that's *not* normal!" I can't resist screeching back. "Your friends might see!"

But all the same, I pull myself to my feet, heaving myself up on a branch. I hop up to Angel, who is eating grass. I push her down into the road and stand on the verge. Then I jump on. Angel puts up her head, a little surprised, but she doesn't seem to mind.

I grab hold of the greasy hair at the base of Angel's neck,
my leg throbbing. Horses have nice flat, comfortable backs, but
cows' backs are bony, with a high ridge running all the way from
neck to tail.

Angel puts on a little spurt as she barges past Samantha and
once more into the lead.

The sun peeps over the horizon and floods the valley with pink and orange light. I feel so tired, all I can do is cling on and hope Angel knows the way home. Kuri runs along beside us, giving me reproachful glances and finally, after what feels like ages, we reach the farm gate. Annabelle flies ahead and opens it. The exhausted cows troop patiently into the yard, one by one. When the last one's in, Annabelle slams the gate and latches it.

We watch as a light comes on and the curtains fly open.

"You're so dead," whispers Annabelle.

The window opens and Dad's dark figure leans out. "Cows are out," he roars. He hesitates. "No, they're *in*," he says in surprise.

There's no way I can cover this up. I'm not even sure if I'm going to be able to get off Angel without someone lifting me, my leg hurts so much.

Then Dad spies Annabelle sitting on the gate. "Annabelle?"

"Ask her," she points at me, her voice carrying across the yard in the pink morning light.

"Hello, Dad," I say quietly, from Angel's back. "Umm ... aren't you going to wish me a happy birthday?"

Chapter 8

As soon as Dad hears that Behemoth plus two wives are in Dottie's garden, he grabs a bucket of cow feed, a rope and Kuri, and belts off in the truck. The cows are tired and sweating heavily. I'm still sitting on Angel. I can't get off. I've gone all stiff and I think I might cry.

The front door flies open and Mum steps into the yard. Her hair is sticking up and she's wearing mismatched wellies. "What's happening?" she asks.

I look at Annabelle. She saw everything. This is her chance to get me into the biggest trouble of my life. I wait for the onslaught.

Annabelle takes a deep breath. "We thought we could bring the cows in on our own," she says.

I'm so surprised I nearly fall off Angel.

"So that Linnie wouldn't miss the bore," Annabelle continues. "But they went the wrong way. We've got them all back, except Lady Porridge, Skylark and ..." She paused. "Behemoth." Mum claps her hand to her mouth. "Do you know where they are now?" she says, letting her hand drop.

"I shut them in Dottie's back garden," I say quietly. I can't believe Annabelle has done this for me. This was her once-in-a-lifetime opportunity to get me into trouble. And she didn't take it.

Quite the reverse. She's *sharing* the blame.

Is she ill?

I rub my leg. I need to get off this cow. I think Angel's fed up with me too. She keeps reaching round and butting my foot with her head.

"All the cows got as far as Dottie's?" asks Mum incredulously.

"We've got them back," says Annabelle firmly.

"What got *into* you, Annabelle?" Mum snaps. "That was incredibly stupid. You know better than that."

"Ow, ow ow," I moan, hoping to take some of the wrath away from my sister.

Mum makes her way over to me. Wordlessly she lifts me off Angel's back. She's strong, my mum. She sets me down on an upturned bucket and rolls up my trouser leg.

"It's bruised, but you'll live," she says. She looks me in the eye. She knows it was all my idea. She knows what I'm like. "*Never* let the cows out into the road," she says. "You could've been killed."

Then she leaves me and starts pushing the weary cows into the lower yard, ready for the vet.

Annabelle looks at me.

"Thanks," I say, in a quiet voice.

"You saved me from Behemoth, so I saved you back," says Annabelle. "Now we're quits." She's about to run off to help Mum, but I grab her arm.

"What was all that stuff about being normal?" I ask.

"You're too young to understand," says Annabelle, annoyingly. But then she sighs and looks hard at me. "It's bad enough that I live on a farm. Everyone says I always have muddy shoes and that my school uniform smells of smoke because Mum insists on drying it by the fire, instead of using the tumble drier like *normal* mothers do. But I can just about get away with it if I don't do anything else to stand out."

I must be looking especially confused because she carries on.

"To be a member of the Three Tops, you have to have the right shoes, the right hair, the right clothes. You must listen to the correct music and like the same people. Anything that's different is *bad*. Like saying the wrong thing, or going to see a stupid river wave instead of going shopping. And chasing a load of cows through town in the middle of the night is *not* normal." Annabelle rubs her neck. She does this when she's worried. "And shutting the bull in Dottie's garden means everyone will know."

"It sounds hard work, being a member of the Three Tops," I say.

"It is," says Annabelle. "We even have to wear the right socks. Dottie notices *everything*. I have to watch myself *all* the time. Even my laugh is too squeaky sometimes, and *you* ..." Her voice trails off.

"Me?" I say brightly.

"You're the opposite of normal," says Annabelle. "You couldn't be a member of the Three Tops in a million years. I get a lot of stick for having such a quirky sister."

"Sorry," I say.

Annabelle shrugs. "It's not really your fault," she mutters, looking away.

I don't have any of these problems. Me and my friend Jenny just hang out and we don't take much notice of what anyone else is doing, unless it looks interesting. And who cares what anyone is wearing? Clothes are for keeping you warm, right?

"Maybe you should get some new friends," I suggest in a small voice.

"It's not as easy as that," snaps Annabelle.

"Or maybe a new sister?"

Annabelle rolls her eyes, but I notice a small but definite lift at the corners of her mouth.

"Can someone help me with the gate, please?" calls Mum from the lower yard, and Annabelle runs off.

I watch her from under my eyebrows. I hadn't realised that being Annabelle was quite so complicated. All this explains why she is so particular about having the right shirt to wear to school, or why she goes bananas if I nick her socks. I thought she was just being a pain.

Actually, I still think she's a pain, but at least now I know there may be a reason for it.

After the cows are safely penned, Mum makes us go in for breakfast. She's not saying much. She's still mad. And, at last, I hear the yard gate open. I hobble to the window and see Behemoth trot into the yard, with the others close behind.

Mum breathes out and goes to the door. "Everything all right?" she calls to Dad.

"There was a bit of damage to the lawn, but nothing too bad," I hear Dad say. "It could have been worse."

Mum goes out of the door and shuts it behind her. She and Dad have a muffled conversation.

I can't help looking at the time. It's eight o'clock in the morning. The bore will occur in one hour. Of course, there's no chance we'll go now.

Mum and Dad come in the kitchen and take off their boots. Both are looking hard at us.

"Right," says Mum, "as a punishment, I want Linnie to clean out the henhouse. I want it scrubbed."

I sigh. This is the worst job on the farm. The chickens make a lot of mess, and sometimes there are horrible rubbery eggs in amongst the poo. It makes me feel sick. But I deserve it, I guess. Letting the cows out just so I could go to the bore was a crazy thing to do.

"And what's my punishment?" asks Annabelle.

Mum and Dad exchange glances. "We're still working on it," says Mum.

This means they definitely know it was all my fault.

"You can do the chickens this afternoon," says Mum. Her face changes. "But right now, you'd better get your shoes on."

I grimace. What evil task has my mother lined up for me now?

"If we rush, we can get to the river in time," she says.

I'm dumbstruck.

"Hurry up before she changes her mind," says Dad. He comes over and kisses the top of my head. "Happy Birthday."

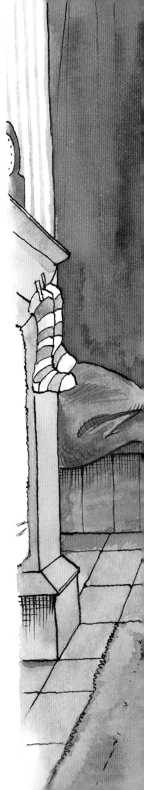

So now I'm running around, finding my coat and shoes, and Annabelle is doing the same. I really don't understand parents. One minute they're doling out the worst punishment in the world, the next they're taking us out on an adventure. Though Dad isn't coming. There's too much to do before the vet comes. And we have to come home the minute the bore has passed us.

"Dottie said you can still go shopping with her," says Dad to Annabelle. "You can do that instead of going to the bore, if you like, seeing how things have changed."

Annabelle pauses, and then she glances sideways at me. "I think I'll go to the river anyway," she says. "Just this once."

Motives

Linnie's path

Why does Linnie leave the house?

Why does Linnie cry?

Why does Linnie let out the cows?

Annabelle's path

Why doesn't Annabelle want to go to the bore?

Why does Annabelle come to help?

Why is Annabelle angr that the cows are in Dottie's garden?

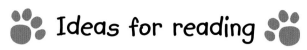

Ideas for reading

Written by Clare Dowdall, PhD
Lecturer and Primary Literacy Consultant

Reading objectives:
- predict what might happen from details stated and implied
- identify and discuss themes and conventions in and across a wide range of writing
- draw inferences such as inferring characters' feelings, thoughts and motives

Spoken language objectives:
- participate in discussions, presentations and role play
- use spoken language to develop understanding through speculating, hypothesising, imagining and exploring ideas

- give well-structured descriptions, explanations and narratives for different purposes, including for expressing feelings
- maintain attention and participate actively in collaborative conversations

Curriculum links: Citizenship; Geography

Interest words: five-star bore, tuberculosis, tsunami, exhilarating, stirks, rampaging, summoning, excruciating, reproachful, incredulously

Resources: paper, pens, internet

Build a context for reading

- Explain that this story is set around a geographical event, a five-star bore, and that a bore is a large wave that comes down a river. Ask if anyone has seen a bore and discuss what they think it would be like to witness such an event.
- Ask children to read the blurb and consider the image on the front cover. Discuss what the narrator's plan may be and what may happen in the story.

Understand and apply reading strategies

- Ask children to read to p9 silently, noting the main themes that are introduced in this chapter, e.g. disappointment and conflict between the sisters.
- Ask children to discuss what they know about the main characters from just the first chapter, e.g. *Linnie is passionate.* Based on this information, ask children to predict how the story might develop and what might happen to Linnie and Annabelle.
- Ask children to read to the end of the book, noting how the author is constructing and building tension and excitement in the story, and what themes are presented.